UNWORLDLY·TRAVELERS
"The Gracious Dinner Guests"

AF427254

UNWORLDLY TRAVELERS
"The Gracious Dinner Guests"
Published by Mansfield Monsters Independent Press
PO Box 7023 Colorado Springs CO 80933

Copyright ©2025 Mansfield Monsters Independent Press
Illustrations Copyright ©2025 Doug Mansfield

Designed and formatted by Doug Mansfield

Unworldly Travelers
Publication Title & Concept by Doug Mansfield

"The Gracious Dinner Guests"
Book Title by Doug Mansfield

ISBN 979-8-9923890-0-5

Story by A. Lukasavige
Book Cover and Illustrations by Doug Mansfield

UNWORLDLY·TRAVELERS

"The Gracious Dinner Guests"

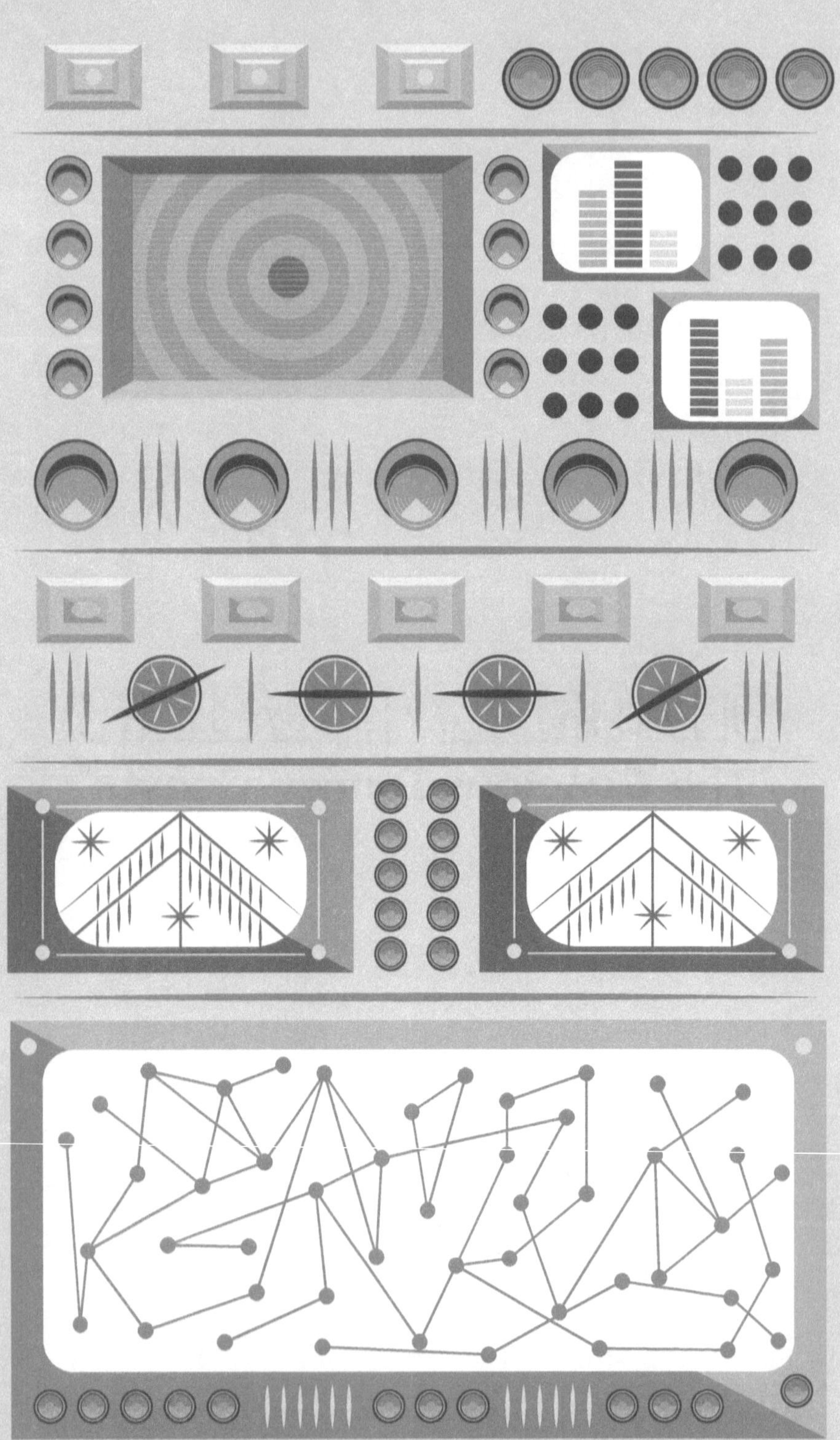

Date: October 17, 5076
Time: 16:23
Location: Somewhere Along An Ancient, Undocumented Asteroid Belt 217 Light years Away From Earth
Status: Unknown
Inquiry No. 1,062

Control Tower: SS Orion, come in. This is control tower three.

SS Orion: SS Orion to control tower three, we copy. This is Stefan. Go ahead.

Control Tower: Nice to hear from you again, Stefan. What is your status?

SS Orion: SS Orion is stable. Food rations are limited, but we will manage until the next station on Planet Thatis. I am sending ship stats over now.

Control Tower: 10-4. I've just received the stats, thank you. Have you sent the updated tracking documents to the research department yet?

SS Orion: Affirmative. Tracking documents were

sent over just before you radioed.

SS Orion: ...dad, when can we-

SS Orion: Shh, Yasmin! I'm in the middle of a radio call. Please go wait with your mother.

SS Orion: CT3, disregard the last message.

Control Tower: Ha ha! Don't worry about it, Stefan. Are you and the family holding up well out there?

SS Orion: As well as we can be. The kids are getting restless. I've tried to assure them we are nearly done with mapping out this asteroid belt, but we keep finding more that needs to be documented out here.

Control Tower: The things we do for science!

Control Tower: Listen, Stefan, I've got to check on the other research ships out there before I go home for the day. I'm going to let you go. I look forward to speaking with you tomorrow!

SS Orion: 10-4. Thank you CT3. Have a nice night. This is SS Orion signing off. Over and out.

Stefan slid his headset off and placed it neatly back onto the shelf beside him. With a heavy sigh, he glanced over the multitude of loose papers scattered around his desk that were filled with the day's research. For nearly six months, Stefan and his family had been cooped up in a small research spaceship to document a newly discovered asteroid belt.

Ever since he was young, Stefan dreamed of exploring the universe just as his ancestors had. He grew up with stories of his late grandfather who was the first human to make contact with an extraterrestrial species. He grew up learning of his grandfather's escapades through the vastness of space which had been previously undiscovered since the beginning of mankind.

In the year 4719, Stefan's grandfather, Noam, was the first man to make contact with aliens. At that time, space travel had become far more normalized within the scientific communities and became much more accessible for researchers to expand their horizons. Noam was the first scientist to be sent into space in the new research-specific spacecraft.

The spacecraft was designed to withstand travel across the galaxy far quicker than any other spaceship with more maneuverability than usual. This allowed the scientists to reach further into space than was ever thought possible. On Noam's first expedition, he ran into a new planet teaming with life. On that planet, he made contact with an alien species called Scizuls.

The discovery was revolutionary in the world of science. It was the first undeniable evidence of life outside of Earth with the capacity to converse with humans. Thankfully for Noam, the Scizuls were a friendly species. They welcomed him to their planet with open arms and told stories about how they awaited the arrival of Humans for thousands of years.

Noam returned to Earth with the new discovery and was named 'The Hero of Science' for his dedication to research on the matter. In the years following the first initial discovery, humans greatly expanded their research vessel fleet and sent dozens of teams out to continue exploration of the universe.

Over the many years of exploration, hundreds of new extraterrestrial species were discovered. While some were unwelcoming to Humans and ordered to be left alone, many were kind and excited for the arrival of Humans. Eventually, the first set of aliens visited Earth. Noam had traveled to and from Planet Vipra many times since his first contact there. He made many friends with the Scizuls during his visits. It took some time, but he was able to persuade some of his closest friends on Planet Vipra to visit Earth and see its beauty.

At first, the Scizuls were wary of visiting Earth. They were afraid of any harsh reactions from Humans. The last thing they wanted was a war to break out between the two populations.

Thankfully, the Humans on Earth welcomed the Scizuls with open arms upon their first arrival. From then on, Scizuls traveled between the two planets frequently. They shared materials from their planet in return for knowledge about Earth, and after only five years, they had named Earth as their second home. No Human would turn their head to stare at a Scizul passing in the street and no hate was spread between

the two species.

Soon enough, Scizuls weren't the only alien life exploring Earth. The Scizuls told other planets of Earth and convinced them to pay the Humans a visit. Earth quickly became a popular place for all alien life to visit because of how welcoming it was. Some even left their planets entirely to move to Earth and start anew.

Ever since Noam made first contact with the Scizuls in 4719, space research was a popular subject among the people. The science field grew exponentially with the desire to explore and discover the unknown.

All his life, Stefan strived to be like his grandfather. He spent his childhood trying his hardest in school so he could get accepted into the most prestigious science university. On his eighteenth birthday, all of his hard work paid off, and an acceptance letter was sent to him that morning. It was the best birthday he ever had.

Stefan's hard work didn't stop there. He spent eight grueling years studying and performing as well as he could in that university. By the time he graduated, Stefan was the top-performing student in the university's history, earning him a spot on the world's finest space research team.

While the position he was put into wasn't fantastic by any means, he took whatever he got with excitement. Anything related to space research was good enough for him.

As the years grew on, Stefan slowly began to climb to higher positions in space research. A year ago, Stefan was promoted to be the head researcher for his very own spacecraft with his wife, Harper, as his assistant. They were given the task of documenting and mapping out an asteroid belt that had just been discovered on a recent satellite scan into deep space.

Stefan met Harper when they were paired together to conduct important research on space debris gathered from several light years away. Their research led to the discovery of the wreckage of a spacecraft from a failed attempt at space travel hundreds of years before—solving the cold-case mystery of SS Nero. From the moment they began their research project together, the two became inseparable.

Eventually, they married and had children of their own which they frequently brought along on their research trips. It came as a surprise when they were scheduled together on their own research spacecraft. While it was a great honor to document space together, it unfortunately meant that their children had to go with them on the journey.

In the beginning, Xander and Yasmin were thrilled for the chance to explore space and meet aliens, but they quickly grew bored with staring out across the mundane expanse of asteroids as their parents mapped out each one they passed by. Of course though, they were still elated whenever the spaceship landed on a new planet to restock on supplies. Somehow, they managed to make at least a dozen friends on each planet they visited, no matter how short of a time they were there.

"Daddd," Yasmin groaned from behind him, tugging at his shirt. "I'm hungry. Are we near any places with actual food?"

Stefan sighed, swiveling his chair around to face his daughter. "Yasmin, I told you this earlier and I will tell you again, we are in the middle of nowhere. We won't reach Planet Thatis until tomorrow. We have food on board."

"But I don't want our food. It's gross and has been sitting there for a month now!"

"Unfortunately that is all we have for right now," Stefan replied with a shrug. "You can either eat the food we have here or wait until we reach Thatis tomorrow."

Stefan stood from his chair and took Yasmin's hands in his own. He spun her around with him and began to lead her out of the control room. Harper waited at the open door for them with a smile on her face.

Before Stefan could make it out of the control room though, a loud beep sounded from one of the many radars equipped aboard the ship. Stefan jumped slightly, not expecting to run into any other life in the middle of the asteroid belt. He quickly turned and ran to look at the anomaly.

In front of him, the heat-detection radar was rapidly beeping as it noted something incredibly close to them. Stefan messed with the controls to try and reset the machine, assuming it was a malfunction. He flicked the 'off' switch and waited several seconds before turning it back on again.

Several quiet seconds dragged by without any noise, so he sighed and turned back to Harper to say, "Remind me to get that checked when we reach Thatis tomorrow. It's–"

Loud, rapid beeping cut off whatever he was going to say next. Alarmed, Stefan turned to stare at the small screen once more. A large blob of heat spread across the center of the screen, noting something almost directly on top of them. He tried to reset the machine again, but each time he reset the radar, the heat anomaly stayed in the same spot.

"What the…" Stefan began, racking his brain for any explanation of the anomaly.

Yasmin gasped from behind him, pointing excitedly out of the font window before asking, "Look! There's a place! Can we go there for dinner? Please?"

Stefan looked up from the radar and out into the deep expanse of space, his eyes widening as he saw what his daughter pointed out. Shockingly, sat atop one of the asteroids, a small building stared back at him. From that distance, he could make out a flickering neon sign that spelled out 'Vruzai's Diner: Open 24/7. All species welcome.'

"What is it?" Harper asked from behind him as she entered the room.

"I don't know…" Stefan responded truthfully. "A diner, apparently. I don't know how the radar didn't detect that before. It just appeared out of nowhere."

"Can we go?!" Yasmin still begged, looking eagerly between her parents.

"I suppose," Stefan shrugged. "I don't see what the harm in that could be."

While it was strange that the diner alluded the heat radar for so long, Stefan wasn't worried. He had encountered many things during his time in space. Things he previously thought to be impossible proved him wrong more times than he could count.

After overriding the ship's autopilot, Stefan steered toward the diner. As they neared, he began the search for a suitable place to land. Thankfully, he didn't have to search long because there were miles of flat ground surrounding the lonely building.

"Where are we going?" Xander, Stefan's son, voiced from behind.

He likely felt the shift of the ship's path. Xander had always been obsessed with the way the spaceship worked and often sat in while Stefan flew around. Earlier, he had been told of their plans to stay on track to Planet Thatis overnight. The dramatic shift away from their path was something Xander definitely did not miss.

"We are stopping for some food," Harper responded as he joined the group.

"What? We aren't supposed to reach Thatis until tomorrow," he noted.

"Yeah, but look!" Yasmin piped up. "There's a restaurant there! Dad said we can stop there for food instead of eating the stuff we have."

"How?" Xander asked, dumbfounded as he viewed the diner out the front window.

"We don't ask questions in space, son," Stefan replied with a laugh. "We just take what we are given. Sit and put on your seatbelt, please. We are about to land."

As soon as Xander was buckled in, Stefan began the procedures to land the ship. With all the technological advancements in recent years, landing the ship wasn't horribly difficult. All he had to do was choose a place to land and the ship's auto-landing function would do the rest of the hard work for him.

Stefan was trained to pilot the ship without the use of autopilot, but whenever possible, he preferred to use the autopilot function. He would do whatever he could to save his brain power for doing research rather than flying a ship.

The landing was smooth and went without any interruptions. As soon as Yasmin put on her gear that protected her from the harsh elements of space, she jumped outside, excited for the meal she was about to have.

Xander was the last to leave the safety of the spaceship. He was still quite apprehensive over the discovery of the mysterious diner. Although he voiced his concerns about eating at the diner, Stefan assured him that it would be alright. He had always been the more cautious family member, afraid of the unexpected. The diner was quiet and empty when they entered. Only the sound of a bell rang through the air as the door swung shut behind them. Behind a corner, a creature stepped out to inspect the source of the sound.

The man in front of them was completely blue and had three eyes that flicked around the room almost as if they were each their own separate being. If Stefan hadn't already been used to the curious way different alien species presented themselves, he would have been terrified of the creature before them. Eventually, all three eyes focused on the family that still stood awkwardly at the entrance.

"Welcome to Vruzai's Diner," the man greeted in a bored tone, almost as if he was annoyed they were there in the first palace. "My name is Vruzai, as is obvious because I'm the only one here. Please sit. I know it'll be hard to find a spot because of how busy the place is, but I assure you that there is an empty table somewhere in this establishment."

Stefan couldn't tell if Vruzai was trying to be funny or not. Similarly, he couldn't tell if the man was serious about the place being busy. There wasn't another soul around for many light years. All he could do was muster up a small laugh and turn his attention away from the strange man.

Yasmin excitedly led the way, unconcerned about the way the man was acting. She sat herself in the middle of a large table and immediately picked up the menu in front of her. The rest followed and took their places beside her.

"What will you have?" Vruzai asked with a sigh. "If you are unable to read the menu, we have nearly anything you could imagine here. Though, I'm unsure how you would have made it here without the ability to read. I would assume the ability to read would be crucial in order to know this was a diner. I mean, for all you know, you could have just walked into someone's murder house."

Stefan grimaced when he watched Xander slowly turn and give him a deadpan stare that screamed 'I told you so.' He hoped the man was just joking.

He had to be joking, right?

Yasmin, who didn't seem to catch onto the worrying statement from Vruzai, waved her hand to get his attention. Vruzai slowly turned to her, one of his eyes staying locked on Stefan.

Vruzai was immediately bombarded with a mirage of dishes from Yasmin who wished to try one of everything. Stefan wasn't sure where she inherited her lack of picky eating from. He couldn't believe some of the things that were on the menu that she wanted to try.

What the hell were fried Aphut lungs??

Xander refused to get anything, saying that everything on the menu looked gross and that he would never trust a sketchy diner in the middle of nowhere. Stefan hissed at him to shut up. Unlike Yasmin, he had always been a picky eater and never failed to voice his opinions on the matter.

Stefan chose to share a meal with Harper. With Yasmin ordering nearly everything on the menu, they couldn't splurge on anything big. They needed to save at least some of their money for the future.

Vruzai left without a word, leaving the family in silence. However, the silence didn't last for long; a jukebox in the corner suddenly shuddered to life with a slow song Stefan couldn't help but recognize. It was the song he had danced to at his wedding with Harper. Stefan smiled at the memory, glad for the coincidence of music

choice.

Strangely though, each song that followed was one Stefan had clear memories of. One song was all the way back from his childhood. It was a song that his grandmother commonly sang to him when he visited. He didn't know it was an actual song. He had never heard it outside the comfort of his grandmother's home.

Even more strangely, the voice sounded far too similar to his Grandmothers. It was as if he was back on Earth sitting around a campfire and singing along as his Grandmother strummed a guitar.

Another song was from his university days. It was a song he used to study along to nearly every day. Every song after that shot him back in time, making him forget where he was.

It was strange, but Stefan did his best to convince himself it was merely a coincidence and sat back to continue enjoying the music. Surely Vruzai just had similar taste in music. There was no way he would have known all those songs Stefan had such a deep connection to.

It was almost as if time worked differently in the diner.

Stefan could have sworn he listened to nearly an hour's worth of music while they waited for their food. The music seemed to make him forget what they were there for.

When he remembered they were meant to be waiting for food, he looked up to find a clock. It had been far too long to wait for their food to be ready.

Had Vruzai forgotten about them?

When Stefan finally found a small clock mounted on the far wall, he furrowed his eyebrows in confusion. It had only been, at most, ten minutes since they first entered Vruzai's diner.

Almost as if Vruzai could read his mind, the blue creature stepped out from what Stefan assumed was the kitchen with a large tray of food. He caught Stefan's gaze with one of his eyes and watched him carefully. Idly, Stefan wondered if Vruzai knew what was going on with the music coincidence and strange jump in time.

The smell of food made him forget about his worries. Plate after plate of food was placed in front of Yasmin. She was elated at the array of dishes in front of her and immediately dug into what

looked like a pile of purple goo. A large bowl of neon green salad was placed between Stefan and Harper along with two sets of utensils. As repulsed as he was at the sight, Stefan took a bite and was surprised when he enjoyed the taste. It reminded him of the foods his mother used to make him in his childhood.

As he ate, it was as if he was transported back into his memories. Stefan couldn't shake the feeling that it wasn't just a coincidence that the food he was served reminded him so much of his childhood. It was just like the music.

How did Vruzai know everything that he loved?

However concerning it was, Stefan wasn't sad that the food tasted as good as it did. He burned through the entire salad with a smile as he listened to his favorite music.

Just as he finished the last bite of salad, he looked over to see how Yasmin was faring with her mirage of dishes. Yasmin and Xander were bickering over a plate of what looked like a kebab of eyeballs and Stefan mentally cringed at the sight. If Yasmin wanted to try an eyeball kebab, he wasn't going to stop her. Weirdly, it looked as though Yasmin had barely touched any of her food. Although it looked like she was scarfing down plate after plate, only two empty plates sat to the side.

Stefan shrugged to himself and turned to Harper. She had a wide smile on her face as she dug around in the bowl of salad before her.

Stefan froze.

Harper dug through… the nearly full bowl of salad before her.

…*What?*

Had he not just finished off the last of it a second ago?

It was then that he realized she had been speaking to him.

"Did you hear me?" Harper asked after swallowing a mouthful of the neon green salad.

"Sorry?" Stefan asked quietly.

"I asked you what you thought of the salad?" Harper repeated. "I haven't seen you take a bite yet."

Stefan glanced down at his hand. He was holding a fork full of salad which hovered between them. Quickly, he shoved the bite of food into his mouth and nodded back at her.

There was no way he had just imagined consuming an entire bowl of salad. It tasted the same as it had before—just like his mother's cooking.

What did she mean she hadn't seen him eat any of it?

He had just finished the whole thing??

"It's good," Stefan responded, his voice muffled by the mouthful of food.

"I agree! Kids, how is your food?" Harper smiled, turning her attention away from him.

"I've never had anything better," Yasmin cheered. "I'm so full now."

Stefan glanced down at her multiple plates of food only to find that they were all completely empty. He swore only a minute ago she had barely begun eating. There was no way she could have eaten all of that food in the short time it took for him to eat a single bite of salad.

When he looked back to his own bowl of food, it too was empty. Hadn't he just taken a bite from a full bowl of salad? Harper sat back with a sigh as she patted her stomach with a content smile. "Well that was good," she said. "We should come here again."

"Yes, please!" Yasmin replied happily. "Oh, no way! There's a dessert menu. I missed that before. Can we please get some dessert?"

"I thought you said you were full a minute ago, Yasmin," Stefan chuckled carefully, unsure if he was going insane or not.

What was this place?

"No. I never said that," Yasmin insisted. "I didn't even eat that much."

Almost on cue, Stefan looked down to see a measly two empty plates in front of his daughter. There was no trace of the dozens of meals Yasmin had ordered earlier that night. It was as if anything he said or thought immediately became untrue.

Whatever the diner was doing to him, Stefan didn't like it because he swore on his life that he had heard Yasmin order everything on that menu. He was ready to get out of the diner and never go back. Something was wrong with that place, but no matter how hard he tried, he couldn't figure out what it was.

Warily, Stefan called Vruzai over and asked for a bill.

"What about dessert?" Yasmin pouted.

"Maybe next time," Stefan said passively as he anxiously waited for Vruzai to make his way over to their table.

"You've already paid, sir," Vruzai spoke calmly.

The creature turned away from Stefan and continued polishing a nearby table.

Had he paid already?

Why couldn't he remember?

All Stefan knew at that point was that he needed to get out. He stood from his chair, the wooden legs scraping against the cold tile floor. Almost immediately, his vision tunneled and he became nauseatingly dizzy.

"Well, I suppose we should head back," Harper said with a yawn. "It's been at least two hours now."

Stefan blinked and he was back in his seat staring at his wife. All he could do was respond with a weak nod. He couldn't believe they had been there for two hours already. He had only taken a single bite of food and yet he was full as if he had eaten the full bowl of salad like he so vividly remembered.

"Y-yeah," Stefan said, clearing his throat, which felt extremely dry all of a sudden. "Let's get out of here."

"Thank you, Mr. Vruzai!" Yasmin's voice sounded from somewhere behind him. "We'll be back soon, I'm sure of it."

Where she was sitting in front of him just a minute ago, an empty chair lay abandoned in her wake. Stefan hadn't heard her get up even once. Somehow, she managed to sneak past him and was already waiting at the door as she conversed with a bored Vruzai.

Slowly, Stefan stood once more, the nauseating feeling still ever-so-present. One of Vruzai's eyes still stared right back at him, watching his every move.

None of his family seemed to notice Stefan's apparent peril in the situation at hand. He watched as they all excitedly geared up to head back to their spacecraft, which, thankfully, still sat right outside the diner where Stefan had originally landed it. With all that had happened that night, Stefan was unsure if their spaceship would still be there.

After they were all ready to go, the family bid Vruzai a final farewell before leaving the diner. Stefan didn't wait to see if Vruzai responded—he wanted to get out of there as fast as possible and back to the safety of the spaceship.

Just before they reached the ship, Stefan felt through his pockets for a key to unlock the loading door. Horrifyingly, he was met with an empty pocket. His heart rapidly picking up pace, Stefan frantically searched his other pockets for the small key, but it was nowhere to be found.

A tap on the glass from one of the diner windows made him jump and he whipped his head around to see what had caused the noise. Vruzai stood at the window with a smile, the key to their spaceship swinging slowly back and forth as he held it up for Stefan to see. Stefan's heart dropped. There was no way he was going back into that diner to retrieve his keys.

"Yasmin," Stefan said, getting his daughter's attention by tapping her shoulder. He continued when she turned to face him. "I seem to have left my keys inside. Could you please go grab them from Mr. Vruzai?"

Yasmin only stared at him in confusion, glancing between him and the diner. A confused frown quickly grew on her face when her eyes finally landed on her father. Slowly, she lifted her hand and pointed to his.

"Dad… you're holding the keys," she responded quietly.

Stefan dropped his gaze to where she pointed. Lo and behold, the small key swung from the keyring around his finger.

No way he had just imagined that. Vruzai just had his keys.

"Ah! You seem to be right. Silly me," Stefan laughed quietly. "Let's head inside."

It took an incredible amount of force to keep himself from repeatedly glancing back to see if Vruzai was still watching him. Stefan could almost *feel* Vruzai's eyes on him as he walked up the ramp. Only when the door was shut and sealed behind him did Stefan finally let out a deep sigh of relief.

He was finally safe.

After putting all of his gear away, he headed to the control room to take off and send their ship back en route to Planet Thatis. With the lack of space traffic, taking off was simple; Stefan didn't need to care about hitting other spaceships in his path.

Soon enough, the spaceship lifted off the ground and began slowly shifting away from Vruzai and his mysterious diner.

"Hey, are you alright, Stefan?" Harper asked when he sat back in his chair with a sigh.

Stefan turned to his wife and gave her a soft smile. "Yes, I'm alright. Just tired."

"Okay," Harper responded quietly. "I'm going to get the kids ready for bed. You head to bed early. Today was long."

Stefan didn't say anything as she left the control room. Instead, he turned his attention out the front window to look at Vruzai's diner once more. Stefan could barely make out the face of Vruzai watching silently as they drifted further apart. Just before Stefan lost sight, he swore he watched the diner vanish before his eyes.

It happened in an instant and if Stefan blinked, he would have missed it. One moment, the diner's flickering led sign blinked through the darkness of space; the next moment, it was gone. There was no trace of the diner.

Quickly, Stefan shot his eyes down to the heat-detecting radar to see if he was imagining things. Much to his surprise, there was no trace of any heat signature on the radar. From his experience, that radar had a detecting distance of well over two hundred miles.

How was it that the diner could vanish and leave no trace whatsoever?

Alarmed, Stefan pulled up the recent logs of the radar. Surely he could find proof that the radar did in fact pick up the diner earlier that evening. Much to his dismay though, the recent logs were empty as if the machine had been off for several hours.

Stefan dug deeper and opened the full log history. While it was harder to read through, it would give all the information, unlike the recent logs. Strangely, no matter how much he searched, there was zero log activity around the time they first laid eyes on Vruzai's diner.

It was as if the diner never existed in the first place.

What…?

Date: October 17, 5076
Time: 20:45
Location: Somewhere Along An Ancient, Undocumented Asteroid Belt 217 Light years Away From Earth
Status: Unknown
Inquiry No. 1,063

SS Orion: CT3, do you copy? This is SS Orion.

...

SS Orion: CT3. Control tower three, do you copy?

Control Tower: This is control tower three. We copy. What are you doing radioing so late? You signed off hours ago, Stefan.

SS Orion: Sorry! I ran into an anomaly on my heat-signature radar a little while ago. I checked the logs so I could document it, but the log doesn't exist. I'm wondering if you can check the logs in your system? Maybe ours is bugging out.

Control Tower: ...strange. I'll take a look. Stand by.

...

Control Tower: SS Orion, do you copy?

SS Orion: Affirmative. Find anything?

Control Tower: No, nothing out of the ordinary. What time did you say this would have been?

SS Orion: Around 16:45, sir.

Control Tower: Huh. Yeah, I'm not seeing anything, Stefan. Must have been your equipment bugging out. Make sure you get that checked out on Planet Thatis tomorrow.

SS Orion: Roger that. I'll have that checked out.

Control Tower: Great. Make sure mechanical hears about that. Over.

SS Orion: 10-4. SS Orion signing off for real this time. Good night. Over and out.

It was official, Stefan was going insane. With the addition of the control tower being unable to see any anomalies on the radar, Stefan was sure he was losing himself.

Had he imagined the entire evening?

He was so sure the diner existed. Stefan felt full, so he must have eaten something, and the only time he remembered eating before Vruzai's Diner was lunch.

"Dad?" Xander's voice murmured from behind Stefan, interrupting his thoughts as he fell closer into madness. "What are you doing?"

Stefan jumped at the sudden intrusion. Harper was meant to put the kids to bed a while ago. Finally, Stefan turned to look at his son who stood in the doorway, a tired look on his face.

"Xander, what are you still doing up?" Stefan smiled, standing up to meet Xander at the door. "Let's go back to bed."

"I heard you out here and wanted to see what you were doing," the boy shrugged.

Stefan sighed and patted Xander's shoulder. "I was just finishing up some work for the night. No need to worry."

Xander searched his father's eyes for a moment, glancing between each of his features as if tracing a map out in his head with what Stefan looked like. Eventually, Xander gave in and let Stefan lead him down the hallway and back to his room. The interaction was strange. It almost felt like Xander was confused about who or what Stefan was by the way he looked at him.

Stefan didn't let himself think about all the possibilities that thought would bring up, so he chalked up the weird interaction to tiredness.

"Sleep well," Stefan whispered as he tucked his son into bed.

Just before he exited the room, chills ran down Stefan's spine.

Horrified, he turned to look back at Xander, only for his blood to run cold when he laid eyes on the bed shrouded in shadow.

What lay on the other side of the room was not his son.

For only a moment, the **thing** lying in his son's bed stared back at him with a look that border lined non-human. The **thing** that looked back at him bore the features of Vruzai for a moment so short that Stefan was sure he imagined it. When he blinked, the sight before him changed. His son was back, but something about him was off.

Slowly, Stefan stepped to one side as he watched his son. At first, there was no reaction from Xander, but suddenly, **one** eye flicked toward him, staring straight into Stefan's soul. Stefan couldn't hide his violent flinch back toward the door.

"Are you alright, Father?" the boy whispered, his voice low and slow as he over-enunciated each syllable.

That was **not** his son's voice and that was **not** how Xander spoke.

His head slowly cocked to the side as he awaited an answer from Stefan. "Is something the matter?"

Stefan could feel his world crumbling beneath him. How he managed to stay upright, he didn't know.

"What… what did you think of Vruzai's diner?" Stefan choked out. His throat was bone-dry.

"It was truly a wonderful establishment. I think we should consider a second visit–"

Stefan didn't stick around to hear the rest of whatever that **thing** in his son's bed had to say. He ran.

With short, panicked breaths, Stefan stumbled down the hallway to his daughter's room, a hand running along the walls to keep him from falling. If he knew one thing and one thing only, he knew Xander hated Vruzai's diner from the moment he first set eyes on it. Xander was far too strong-willed to change his mind over something like that.

What had Vruzai done to him?

What had Vruzai done to them?

Stefan needed to see his daughter to confirm his suspicions, but when he reached Yasmin's room, she was nowhere to be seen. Slowly, Stefan circled the room in hopes she was simply hiding from him, but he had no luck. Yasmin was gone.

It was a horrifying realization. Yasmin never left to venture around the spaceship alone at night. Moreover, she would never sneak out without telling anyone where she went.

After a moment of stunned silence, Stefan stumbled out of his daughter's room and began his search. She had to be on the ship somewhere. He watched Yasmin board the ship before him after they left Vruzai's diner.

The kitchen was empty and so was the kid's homeschooling area—the two most likely places for her to be. He checked the bathrooms and all of the spare bedrooms with no results.

Where was she?

The only place Stefan had yet to check was the control room which he had foolishly left unlocked when he took Xander back to bed. Through the slightly ajar door, Stefan could see the silhouette of his daughter sitting in the control seat and pressing as many buttons as she could.

"Yasmin!" Stefan shouted as he barged through the door. "What did I tell you about messing with the controls?!"

She didn't respond.

At the beginning of their research trip, Yasmin was obsessed with all the gadgets on the control dashboard. There were several times when she was caught messing with controls while nobody was watching. She had been scolded many times over the matter and Stefan assumed she had finally gotten over it. He was wrong.

"Yasmin!" Stefan shouted again as he neared the seat.

Slowly, Yasmin turned in the chair to face him, a blank look on her face that made him stop in his tracks.

"It seems he has arrived," Yasmin whispered. She was wearing the headset and radioing **somebody.**

Exasperated, Stefan tore the headset off of Yasmin's head and put it on to apologize to whomever she was speaking with.

Date: October 17, 5076
Time: 21:05
Location: Somewhere Along An Ancient, Undocumented Asteroid Belt 217 Light years Away From Earth
Status: Unknown
Inquiry No. ????

SS Orion: Hello? Is this thing working? It's me. Do you copy?

????: Haha! It is working. I copy. Go ahead.

SS Orion: Sorry this thing is weird to operate. I'll get the hang of it soon. I have control of the ship. I am working on rerouting it to Rebus Station now.

????: Wonderful. How is the Human?

SS Orion: Oblivious. He's putting the Xander mimic to bed now.

????: Splendid. He will make a wonderful addition to the Rebus Project.

SS Orion: I agree. We haven't seen a human of this caliber in—

SS Orion: ...It seems he has arrived.

...

SS Orion: Hello? This is SS Orion speaking. Do you copy?!

????: I do.

SS Orion: Hi! I'm sorry. My daughter snuck into the control room and got to the headset. I apologize for the interruption.

????: My, it is more than ok, Stefan.

...

SS Orion: Thank you for understanding. I promise I'm trying to teach h– ...who am I speaking with? Why do you know my name?

????: Who I am is of no importance. We will meet soon enough.

SS Orion: What do you mean? Who is this?!

????: Goodbye Stefan.

Stefan tried to radio the mysterious man several times but was met with no response. Finally, he gave up and returned the headset to its place on the shelf. It was then that he realized the spaceship had shifted course. It was heading back in the direction they just came from.

"What the…" Stefan murmured, his eyebrows furrowing as he scanned the dashboard of controls to figure out what caused the reroute. "Yasmin, what did you press?"

Stefan turned to look at her.

Yasmin stood behind him, a wide smile on her face as she responded in a sing-songy voice, "Just the controls necessary to steer us in the right direction~!"

Stefan stilled, his hand freezing on the screen before him. He watched as she swayed happily back and forth as she held eye contact.

"What did you do, Yasmin?" Stefan asked again, this time far more stern.

"Please step away from the controls, Stefan," another voice spoke from the doorway. Stefan looked up to see Harper staring back at him.

What?

Stefan couldn't move.

It was wrong.

All of it was wrong.

"What did you do with my family?" Stefan asked quietly.

"What we did to them is none of your concern. Now please, step away from the controls."

"What is this?! Who are you?! **What** are you?!"

Whatever it was that looked like his wife slowly slid her way across the room until she stood directly in front of him. With a clammy hand, the Harper look-a-like curled her fingers around Stefan's wrist and pulled it off of the dashboard. Panicked, Stefan tried to resist, but the creature held fast with near superhuman-level strength.

It was hopeless.

He tried reaching for his headset to call for help, but the Yasmin look-a-like beat him to it and slid the headset back over her head. She flicked her eyes over to him once before continuing to speak with the same person from before.

When another set of hands grabbed him from behind, Stefan jumped. Before he knew it, his hands were tied behind his back and he was sat at the back of the room with nothing to do but watch his ship get taken over.

"Why?" Stefan asked desperately after several minutes of silence.

It took a while before any of them acknowledged his existence and turned away from their task to face him.

"It's been many years since we've been able to bring a superior human back to Rebus. No ship has ventured into that asteroid belt in years," one of them explained with a shrug. "The last human died before we could make any significant progress."

"Progress for **what**? Please, I just want to go back to my family."

"I'm afraid it's much too late for that, Stefan. They have already been dealt with at this point," the other one chuckled. "We thank you for your sacrifice to the Project."

"What project? What are you doing to me?" Stefan was getting desperate.

He didn't get another response; instead, one of the creatures reached into a small case to pull out an unknown object. At the angle Stefan was at, he couldn't tell what it had just grabbed.

"You talk too much," one said, turning back to the controls with

a groan.

Stefan glanced at the one who spoke, then shifted his attention to the other, who was now slowly nearing him, a hand behind its back with whatever it had just pulled from the case. Confused, and filled with worry, Stefan pushed himself further into the wall in an attempt to get away from the strange creature, but there was nowhere he could go.

Finally, the creature pulled the object out from behind its back. The glint of metal and realization of what was about to happen had his heart rapidly picking up pace.

"No! Please!" he begged, leaning as far away as he could.

"The less you move, the less it will hurt," the creature at the controls grumbled. "You Humans are always so whiny."

A sharp poke at his neck had Stefan jerking back in surprise, which only made the pain worse. Almost immediately, Stefan could feel his eyes drooping closed no matter how hard he tried to keep them open. He could feel his muscles stop responding as he slid further down the wall until he was lying sideways on the cold tiled floor.

"Sleep well, Stefan," the creature smiled.

The last thing he heard was soft laughter from the two creatures fading away as he slipped into unconsciousness.

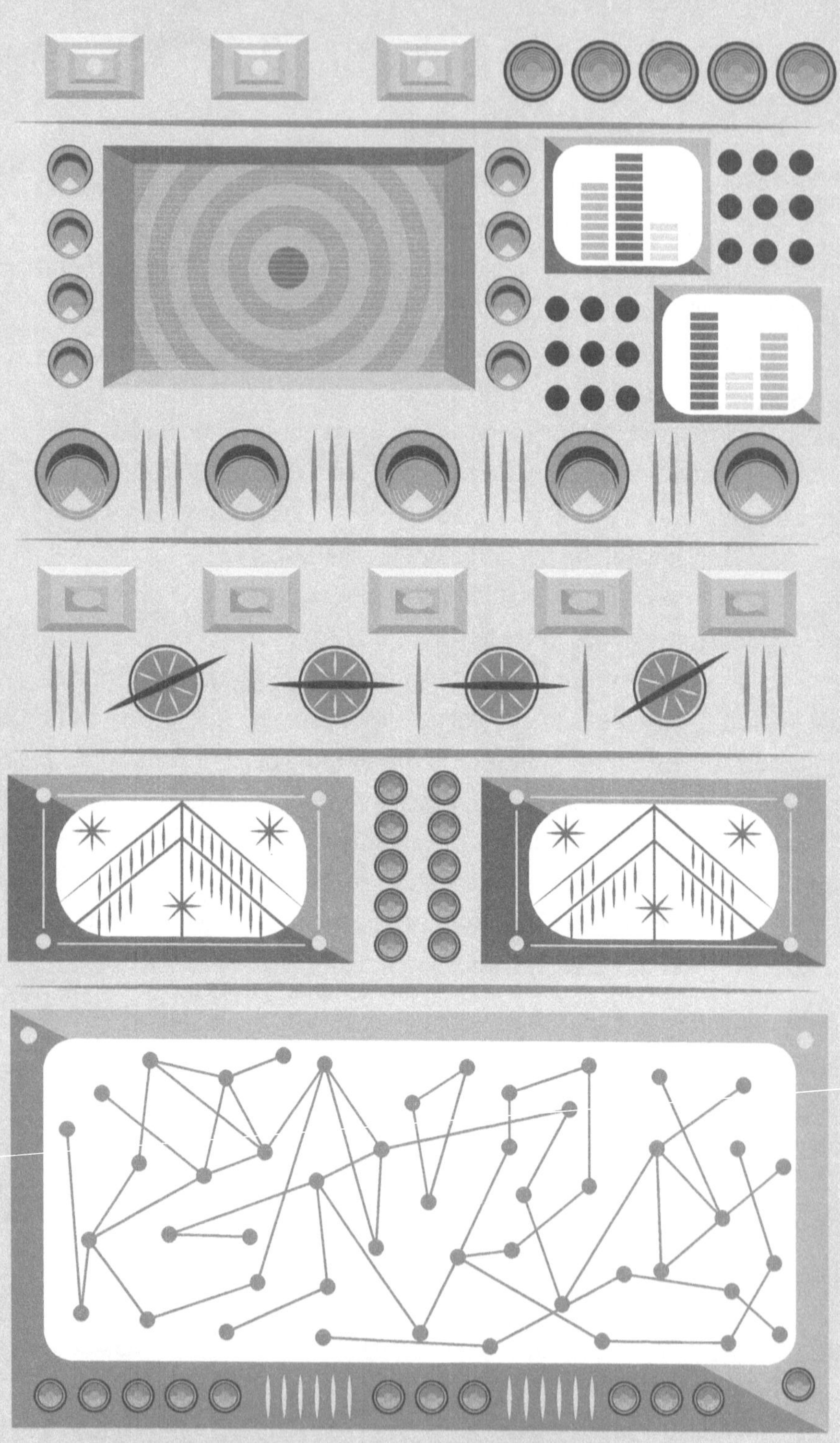